Home

love

SWEET

For all of Charlotte's and Gwen's
great-grandbabies—*J.H.*

For Christy, smart, hardworking, and
wonderful agent plus mentor—*L.W.*

When You Were New
Text copyright © 2023 by Jennifer Harris
Illustrations copyright © 2023 by Lenny Wen
All rights reserved. Manufactured in Italy.

No part of this book may be used or reproduced in any manner whatsoever without written permission
except in the case of brief quotations embodied in critical articles and reviews. For information address
HarperCollins Children's Books, a division of HarperCollins Publishers, 195 Broadway, New York, NY 10007.
www.harpercollinschildrens.com

Library of Congress Control Number: 2021941521
ISBN 978-0-06-313719-6

The artist used gouache, colored pencil, and Adobe Photoshop to create the digital illustrations for this book.
Typography by Chelsea C. Donaldson
22 23 24 25 26 RTLO 10 9 8 7 6 5 4 3 2 1

First Edition

When You Were New

By Jennifer Harris

Illustrated by Lenny Wen

HARPER

An Imprint of HarperCollinsPublishers

When you were new,
there were things you didn't know.

Important things,
like birds sing loudest in the morning
and summer doesn't last forever.

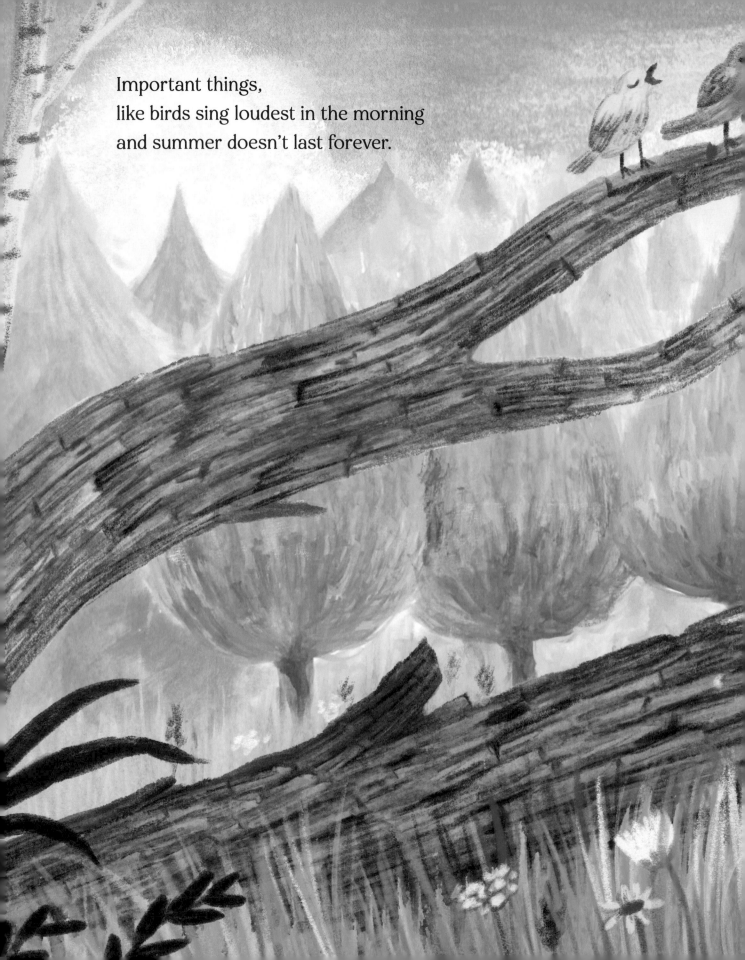

When you were new,
you didn't know cuddles smell different at the beach,
like coconut and salt and sand.

And that sometimes you peel yourself out of them,
and other times you lean into them,
cocooned in the weight of a wet towel.

You didn't know you can't eat the rind of an orange

or that it's difficult to pick raspberries
without eating at least one . . .

or five . . . okay, maybe most of them . . .

and to be still around bees,
because they just need to be bees
and we need to let them do that.

There are things you've forgotten,
so I will remember for you.

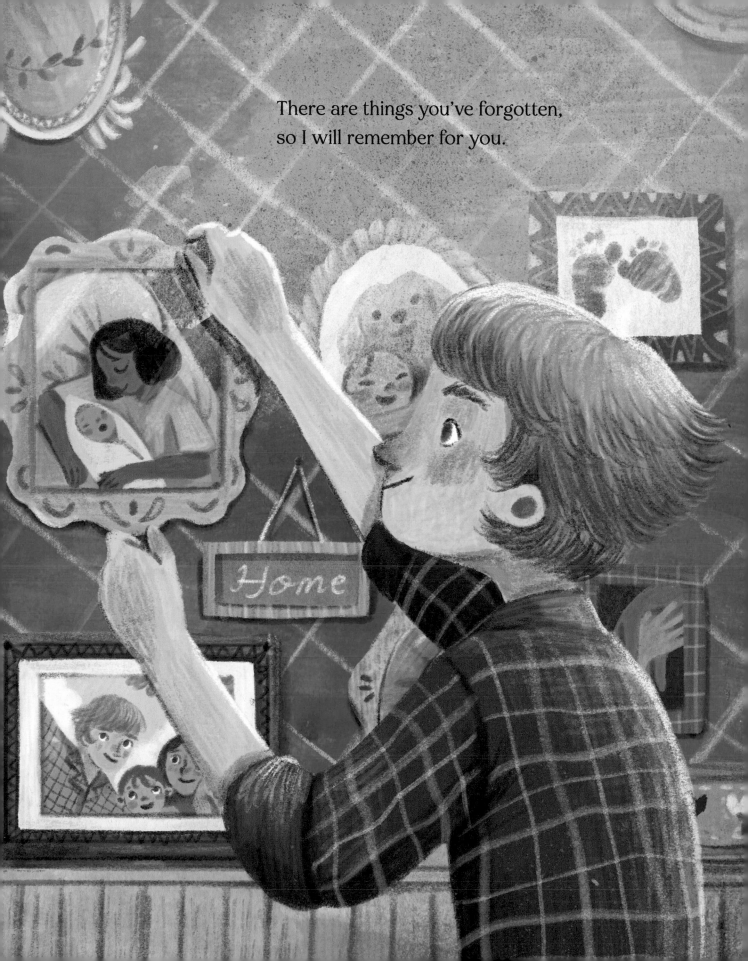

Like how the dog decided you were his,
pressed his grassy paws against you,
and nuzzled your cheek with a little lick

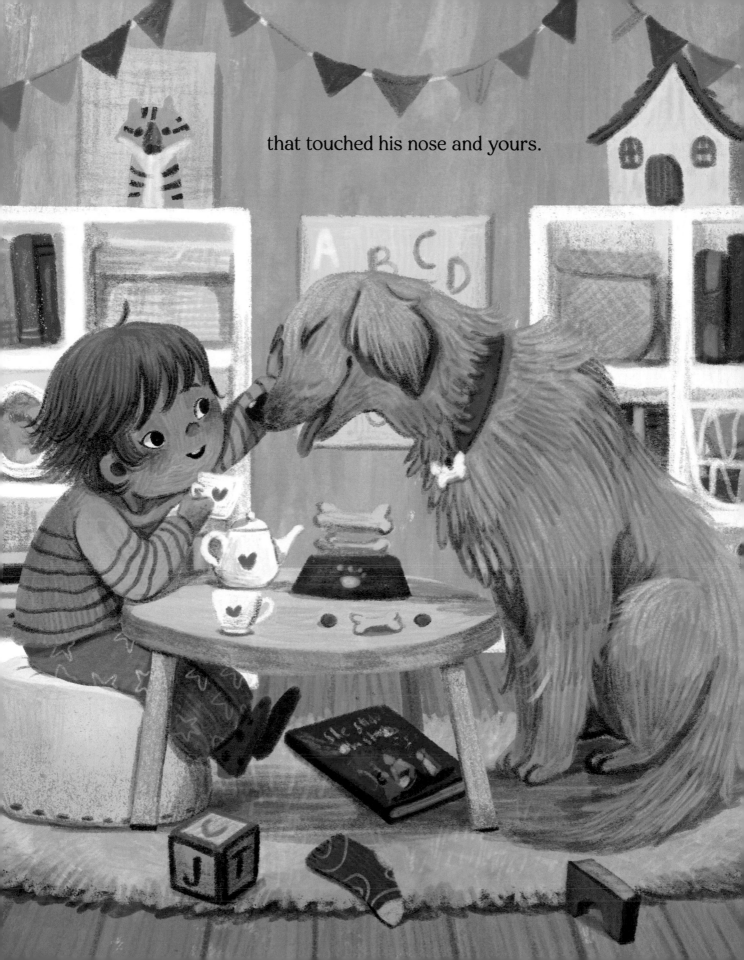

that touched his nose and yours.

And how you would reward him with lost crackers
and all your attention on the laziest afternoons.

When you were new,
you didn't know that when you fall
asleep in a car . . .

and wake up somewhere else,
it isn't because cars are magic.

Or there's always one more story aching to be read.

When you were new,
you didn't know that no matter how
far you travel in this world,

my love will stay with you.

Whenever you need it, it will be there,
all day, all night, all year . . .

forever.